KLAUS BAUMGART lives with his family in Berlin.
The LAURA'S STAR series has had multi-million sales
worldwide, and has been broadcast on TV throughout
Europe, including in the UK. Klaus Baumgart was the
first German author/illustrator to be shortlisted for the
Children's Book Award in 1999 for LAURA'S STAR.

Also available in the LAURA'S STAR series
by Klaus Baumgart

LAURA'S STAR
LAURA'S CHRISTMAS STAR
LAURA'S SECRET

LITTLE TIGER PRESS
An imprint of Magi Publications
1 The Coda Centre, 189 Munster Road, London SW6 6AW
www.littletigerpress.com

First published in Great Britain 2004
Originally published in Germany 2003
by Baumhaus Verlag, Frankfurt

ISBNs 1 84506 036 9 (HB)
1 84506 041 5 (PB)

Printed in China

2 4 6 8 10 9 7 5 3

Laura's Star

and the New Teacher

Klaus Baumgart

English text by Fiona Waters

Little Tiger Press
London

Back to School

Laura hopped from foot to foot in excitement.

"Tomorrow is the first day of term at school," she said happily to the shop assistant. "I am going into a new class *and* I have a new teacher!"

Laura and her dad were shopping for a new schoolbag.

"I need a nice bag, with lots of room for my pens and pencils," said Laura.

"A good, strong bag," said Laura's dad, and sneezed loudly. He had a terrible cold.

Tommy, Laura's little brother, was getting very bored watching Laura trying to make up her mind between the sparkly bags and stripy bags and spotty bags.

"I want a bag too!" he cried.

"You can't have a bag," said Laura. "You don't go to school yet."

"I want one anyway," whinged Tommy.

"Don't start," said Dad. And he sneezed again.

Laura finally decided on a
blue bag with big yellow
stars. It was brilliant! It
had lots of room inside
for all her pens and
pencils so she
was happy.

And the stars reminded her of her friend, the star. Laura's star was her special secret. They had been friends for a long time, but no one else knew.

Laura smiled at Tommy, who was still looking rather grumpy.

"Would you like to carry my new bag home, Tommy?" she asked. Smiling, Tommy took the bag, and they set off.

*   *   *

On the way home, Laura saw her friend, Sophie, in the park and raced over to chat.

"Are you ready for school tomorrow?" Laura asked, excitedly. "Show Sophie my bag, Tommy!"

"Super new bag, Laura!" smiled Sophie. "I packed my bag this morning, so I'm all ready for tomorrow. I can't wait!"

"Me neither," said Laura.

"You two are really stupid. Fancy looking forward to going back to school," said a loud voice.

It was Joe West. Neither Laura nor Sophie liked Joe very much. He was always showing off, and he was a bit of a bully.

"So who is your new teacher?" he asked.

"Mrs Williamson," said Sophie quietly.

"Mrs Williamson! Oooh! She is so scary!" crowed Joe. "She's really strict and she gives out masses of homework."

"How do you know that?" asked Laura.

"Because she was my teacher last year," said Joe with a smirk. "You two had better watch out!" And he walked off, grinning.

"Do you think he's telling the truth?" asked Laura, worried.

"Pooh, I don't think so," said Sophie, but she didn't sound too sure.

"Shall we meet tomorrow in front of the school gate?" asked Laura.

Sophie nodded and then she ran off home. Tommy and Laura walked home slowly. Tommy gave Laura back her bag. "I don't think I want to go to school if the teachers are so scary," he said quietly.

 **A Strange Feeling**

Dad made a toasted cheese and
tomato sandwich for supper,
Laura's favourite. But she didn't
feel very hungry now.

"Laura, are you scared about
going to school?" asked Tommy.
"Do you think Joe was telling the
truth?"

Laura was scared but she said

bravely, "No, I'm sure Joe is just making it up to worry us."

"Will you still be able to play with me if you have so much homework to do?" asked Tommy sadly.

"Of course I'll still play with you," replied Laura, smiling at her little brother. But suppose Joe was telling the truth? Mrs Williamson did sound scary.

Laura had a funny feeling inside her tummy, and she began to think that perhaps she would rather not go to school tomorrow after all.

She wished it was dark already so she could go and talk to her star. Her star always knew how to make things better.

Just then the phone rang. It was Mum! She was staying in London, playing her cello in a concert. Laura and Tommy raced for the phone.

"Laura's new teacher is the worst in the school!" Tommy shouted.

"Who told you that?" asked Mum.

"Joe West," said Laura.

"But you know that Joe makes up stupid stories, Laura," said Mum. "I hope you didn't believe him?"

"Well . . ." answered Laura.

"I am sure your new teacher will be very nice," Mum said confidently.

"Do you really think so?" asked Laura.

"I do! Now let me talk to Dad, and you go to bed and sleep well," said Mum. "I'm sure you will have a lovely day tomorrow."

Dad was looking very sorry for himself indeed. He snuffled and coughed as he talked to Mum.

"Yes. Yes, that's right . . . No. No, I don't think I will be well enough. I shall ask Sophie's mum to take them both . . . All right . . . Yes, we all look forward to seeing you tomorrow evening," and Dad put the phone down with a great sneeze.

"I am not feeling at all well," he said. "I'll have to ask Sophie's mum if she can take you to school tomorrow, Laura." And he shuffled off to bed.

Tommy looked at Laura anxiously. "I wouldn't want to meet

that Mrs Williamson without Dad," he cried.

"No," said Laura. "I don't want that either. He must get better by tomorrow!" She thought for a moment. "Whenever we get sick, Dad brings us a hot lemon drink and a damp cloth to mop our foreheads. Let's do the same for him! That'll make him better!"

Tommy raced into the bathroom, and Laura went back into the kitchen.

Laura squeezed three lemons into Dad's mug and then poured hot water on top. She tasted it. Bleagh! It was really sour. Then she remembered. Sugar! Dad used to add sugar. She added eight spoonfuls, and tasted it again. That was much better!

Tommy skidded into the kitchen with a dripping towel in his hands.

But just at that moment Dad walked in. He took one look at the mess on the table, and the water over the floor, and he groaned.

"Don't worry!" cried Laura. "We'll clean up!"

"We're going to take care of you!" added Tommy importantly.

They tucked Dad up in bed and put the hot lemon drink on his bedside table.

Dad still looked very hot and flushed, but he promised Laura that he would try to take her to school the next morning.

"Promise?" asked Laura.

"Promise," said Dad.

Laura and Tommy mopped up
the kitchen and did the washing up,
and then they said goodnight. At
long last it was time for bed.

# Laura's Star

Laura stood by her window and
looked out into the quiet night. She
didn't feel at all sleepy. She knew
that she needed a good night's sleep
to be ready for school in the
morning but she was too worried
to close her eyes yet.

She looked up at the dark sky,
and there in the midst of all the

twinkling stars was her own very special star!

Laura waved and the star twinkled down at her.

"Oh star, what am I going to do? I start school again tomorrow in a new classroom and with a new teacher. And Joe West says she's very strict and gives tons of homework! And now Dad is sick and probably won't be able to take me to school . . . and Mum is away in London until tomorrow night and . . ." and Laura gulped.

Laura was still frightened even though Mum had told her to ignore what Joe had said. She looked up in the sky again. Oh! Where was her

special star? It had gone! It was no
longer twinkling down at her!

Laura squeezed her eyes tightly
shut so that she wouldn't cry. Then
she felt a breeze against her cheek.
When she opened her eyes there
was her star, filling the whole room
with light!

The star swooped round the room, showering sparkles as it went.

"Oh star, I'm so pleased you're here. You make me feel so much braver," laughed Laura.

Laura's star danced round the room. It dropped a trail of sparkles over her clothes which were hanging up neatly, ready for the morning. It twirled and spun through the air, and hovered over her shoes which Dad had polished so they were extra shiny. Then it flitted over to her lovely new bag, glowing brightly.

Laura giggled. "If only you could come to school with me tomorrow!" she said. "With you there I know I could be brave."

The star did a few spangly
cartwheels round the room, and then
slipped into the new bag. It shone
out between the pencils and the
exercise books.

It gave Laura a fantastic idea.

"You could hide in my new schoolbag, and then you would be there in class with me! That would be wonderful!"

The star twinkled brightly.

Laura tucked her woolly hat into the bag to make it cosy, and the star settled down.

"Time for us both to go to bed,"

whispered Laura, smiling sleepily.
"Goodnight, star."

And before long all was quiet in the house.

The First Day

The next morning Laura leapt out
of bed bright and early. She looked
at her schoolbag. The star wasn't
glowing any more, but she knew it
was there. She dressed quickly and
ran into the kitchen. Dad was
drinking a mug of tea.

"Are you still sick, Dad?" she
asked him anxiously. "Will you be

able to take me to school?"

Dad sneezed, then grinned. "I am feeling a bit better this morning. Anyway, I did promise I would take you to school, so I will," he said.

Tommy stumbled in, looking sleepy, and they all had breakfast together. Laura munched on her cereal and chattered to Tommy. Everything was going to be fine.

Dad smiled at Laura over the top of his mug. "Are you ready, then?" he said. "Come on, Tommy. It's time to take your sister to school."

"Are you still scared, Laura?" Tommy asked.

Laura looked at her schoolbag and thought of her star. "Not now," she said with a smile.

They set off together and walked down the street. Laura saw lots of her friends walking to school with their families, talking and giggling.

But when they reached the school gates, there was no sign of Sophie or her mum.

"Maybe they've gone inside already," said Dad.

"But she promised to wait and meet me here," said Laura crossly.

More and more children came in the gates but still there was no sign of Sophie. Joe West ran in but he didn't even look at Laura.

Dad looked at his watch.

"If Sophie and her mum don't come soon you'll be late," he muttered.

Laura was getting very anxious. What if Mrs Williamson was really cross because they were late?

"Come on, Laura," said Dad finally. "We need to go inside now."

"But Dad, I promised Sophie I would wait for her," pleaded Laura.

She didn't know what to do, but just then Tommy called out, "Here they are!"

Sophie and her mum came dashing down the street.

"There you are!" shrieked Laura. "Come on, we are going to be dreadfully late!"

But Sophie didn't budge.

"I don't want to go in," she cried. "Mrs Williamson is horrid and mean and gives tons of homework."

"Sophie, this is nonsense," said her mum crossly. "I'm sure that Mrs Williamson is lovely. Now I must go. I have to get to work too!"

"Is Sophie afraid?" asked Tommy.

Laura nodded. She realised that Sophie *was* afraid. Maybe Mrs Williamson was as terrible as Joe had said!

Suddenly Laura felt afraid too. But then she felt her star, her special star, leap in her schoolbag. She took Sophie by the hand and said, "Come on! We'll go in together."

Sophie gulped. Her mum looked at her anxiously.

Laura's dad smiled at Sophie's mum. "Don't worry, I'll take Sophie and Laura into school, and I'll make sure they end up in the right classroom," he said.

Sophie's mum gave Sophie a kiss and rushed off.

Laura and Sophie looked at each other, then followed Laura's dad into the school.

A Real Muddle

But it wasn't very easy to find the right classroom. And there didn't seem to be anyone to ask. They walked up and down a great many corridors before they finally found the classroom.

"Wow! This place is huge!" cried Tommy.

Dad stuck his head round the classroom door. Laura squeezed Sophie's hand tightly, then they followed Dad into the room.

The classroom was full of children, but there was no sign of Mrs Williamson.

"Well girls, here you are," said Dad. "Why don't you settle down and I'll go and find Mrs Williamson and tell her you're here."

He hugged Laura and, with a cheery wave to Sophie, he rushed off with Tommy.

Laura and Sophie looked round. Nearly all the desks were taken but there were two empty seats in the front row so they sat down. The girl at the next desk smiled so Laura leant over and asked what they should do.

"Mrs Williamson said we should all sit quietly and draw," said the girl.

"Great! I love drawing," said Laura and she bent down to get her pencils out of her schoolbag.

"Eeek!" she said. There, looking up at her, was a little brown mouse!

"Oh!" cried the girl at the next desk. "That's Toffee, the class mouse. He must have escaped!"

Several children crowded round
and they all started talking at once.
Toffee scuttled back and forth
across the classroom.

Laura felt very sorry for Toffee with all the noise and big feet stomping about. Some children were chasing him, trying to catch him, while others screamed and leapt on to their desks.

Everyone was running about now, and there was a lot of shouting and laughter as Toffee ran up the side of a bookcase and on to the top shelf. He hid there, looking scared.

Poor Toffee! Laura was very worried about getting into trouble, but someone had to rescue him! What could she do?

She gazed down at her bag and saw her star tucked inside, and suddenly she felt brave again.

Laura walked to Mrs Williamson's desk and climbed up on top of it. Standing on her tiptoes she gently reached out towards the little mouse.

"Come on, Toffee," she whispered. "Don't be frightened."

Just as her fingers touched the tip of Toffee's tail, a great silence fell in the classroom. Laura froze.

The door had opened and
someone had walked in. It was
Mrs Williamson!

Mrs Williamson

Mrs Williamson stopped by her desk and looked at Laura in surprise.

"What are you doing standing on my desk?" she asked.

Laura stammered. "I – I was trying to catch Toffee. He's climbed up the bookcase on to the top shelf."

Mrs Williamson frowned.

"Who let him out of his cage?"

"I don't know," whispered Laura, sure that she was in deep trouble. Everyone was silent now, looking at her. She bit her lip, determined not to cry.

Mrs Williamson reached up, cupped her hands round Toffee and gently lifted him down.

Then she smiled as Laura
scrambled down off the desk.

"Thank you for trying to rescue
him. You are a very kind little girl,"
Mrs Williamson said.

Laura and Sophie looked at each
other. Mrs Williamson seemed very
nice. Perhaps Joe West *had* been
telling fibs!

"Now then, children," said Mrs Williamson, "I would like you all to do me a very special drawing. I will pin the best one up on the wall."

Laura sat down, smiling with relief and happiness. She looked down in her schoolbag. One tip of her star was just peeping out from under her hat, winking at her. Everything was fine!

Laura grinned. She knew exactly what she was going to draw for Mrs Williamson.

Everyone was very busy drawing. The girl next to Laura drew Toffee. The boy next to Sophie drew a space rocket.

Laura drew a picture of lots and lots of stars. In the very middle she put the biggest star of all, her own special star.

When they had finished drawing, Mrs Williamson put everyone's picture on the wall because she said they were all so good.

* * *

Before they knew it, Laura and Sophie were walking home with Dad, Tommy and Sophie's mum.

"So, how was your day with Mrs Williamson?" asked Dad.

"Great!" said Laura.

"Great!" said Sophie.

"And how much homework have you got?" asked Tommy.

"None!" chorused Laura and Sophie. "Mrs Williamson is the best teacher in the world!"

At supper that night, Laura told Dad and Tommy all about her exciting day. Then her mum arrived, and Laura had to tell her all about it too. Afterwards she took

her schoolbag up into her bedroom.

"Thank you for being with me today, star," smiled Laura. "You really are my very best friend."

She carried the star to the window and held out her arms.

The star floated out of the window and, with a final shower of sparkles, it flew high up into the sky.

"Goodbye, star," called Laura. "See you again soon!"

And happily Laura snuggled into bed, looking forward to another lovely day at school tomorrow.